Modern Curriculum Press
BEGINNING
TO
READ
Series

Come to School, Dear Dragon

Margaret Hillert

Illustrated by David Helton

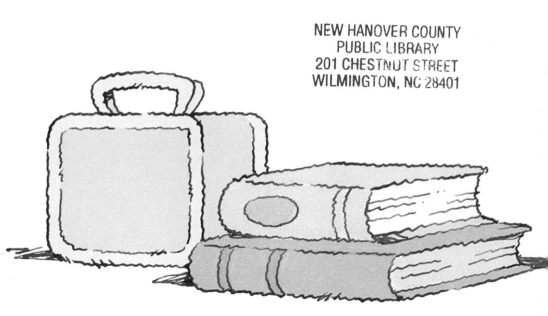

ISBN: 0-8136-5633-8
Printed in the United States of America

20 21 22 23 24 25   06 05 04 03 02

Modern
Curriculum
Press

Pearson Learning Group

1-800-321-3106
www.pearsonlearning.com

Oh, Father.
This is good.
And it is good for me.

Now I have to go.
I want this —
    and this —
        and this.

I have to go now.
I have work to do.
Away I go.
Away, away, away.

Come on.
You can come with me.
Run, run, run.

This is the spot.
I will go in here.
You can not come in,
but do not go away.
I will come out.

I like it here.
I see my friends.
We have work to do, but
we have fun, too.

We work and we play and
we have fun here.

Oh, what is this?
Why are you here?
Why did you come in?

14

You will have to sit down.

Sit, sit.

That is good.

15

I guess you can help us.
Yes, yes.
You can help.

We will make something.
It will look like you.
Yes, you are a help to us.

Here is a book.
Books are fun to read.
We like to read books.

And look at this.
Look in here.
This one looks something
like you.

Now we will go out.
We will go out to play.
Come on out with me.

21

You can help us.

Here is something you can do.

You are a big help.

Here are three balls.
One, two, three balls.
Red, yellow, and blue.
We will play with the balls.

Do this for us.

Help us with this.

We want to play this way.

25

Now we will go.

We can walk with friends.

It is good to have friends.

27

We have to stop here.
Stop and look.
Look out for cars.

Here we go.
This way. This way.
On the way to Father.
Father will have something
good for us to eat.

Here you are with me.
And here I am with you.
Oh, what a good day, dear dragon.

Margaret Hillert, author and poet, has written many books for young readers. She is a former first-grade teacher and lives in Birmingham, Michigan.

Come to School, Dear Dragon uses the 75 words listed below.

a	Father	me	that
am	for	my	the
and	friends		this
are	fun	not	three
at		now	to
away	go		too
	good	oh	two
balls	guess	on	
big		one	us
blue	have	out	
book	help		walk
but	here	play	want
			way
can	I	read	we
cars	in	red	what
come	is	run	why
	it		will
day		see	with
dear	look	sit	work
did	like	something	
do		spot	yellow
down	make	stop	yes
dragon			you
eat			

MG   12/03